W9-AZZ-402

For my sister Janet, who understands geese and children

JOEL AND THE WILD GOOSE

By Helga Sandburg Illustrated by Thomas Daly

The DIAL PRESS New York

 Library of Congress Catalog Card Number: 63-17886 Manufactured in the United States of America

J
Sandburg

Ga News 3.49 net
11/16/65

Breakfast was over. Joel stood at the window. There was no sun. The snowflakes came, soft and slow.

Joel was empty inside. He was lonely. He looked at the gray sky. He thought, "I wonder if they can fly in a sky like that!" The storm was early this year. Only a few bands of wild geese had flown over.

Joel's father was walking around the barnyard where the cows stood. Joel's mother was clattering dishes in the kitchen. She was singing a song to her cats:

Down in the valley, the mockingbird wings,
Telling my story, here's what he sings!

Joel went to lean in the doorway. He said, "What falls and never gets hurt?"

Mother stopped singing. She bent to pet one of her cats.

"Why do you always ask riddles?" She smiled at Joel. "Who knows?"

"The snow," Joel said, without smiling. He went for his galoshes.

"I haven't seen you laugh today, Joel," Mother said. "Are you sad?"

Joel kept pulling on his galoshes. "I can't answer," he thought. He buttoned his coat and got his new stocking cap and went to the door.

"You forgot your mittens," said Mother.

He came back for them. "What goes up and never goes down?"

But Mother was singing her song to her cats. She wasn't listening to Joel:

Down in the valley, the valley so low,
Hang your head over, hear the train blow!

Joel went out into the cold. He told himself the answer, "Your age."

He scuffed the snow with his boots. He blew into the air, making steam with his breath. He sighed. Joel had nothing that was his own. Mother had cats and a flock of chickens. Father had a dog and a great herd of cows and a barnful of pigs.

Joel's brother Jim, who was six years older, had two milk goats and four ducks who lived in a little shed. Last spring Jim had offered two of the ducks to Joel. "But I don't want ducks like Jim. So I have nothing."

Joel said:

I wish a wish, a great big wish,
I wish a wish, I do.
I wish a wish, an enormous wish,
I wish my wish to come true!

He walked past the chicken coop. His mother's hens were scratching for grain in the straw. "Cook-cook-coooooook!" One laid an egg and shouted, "Cut! Cut, cudah! Cut!"

Joel went past the barnyard. In the falling snow the cows did not move their legs. They turned their heads around. "Mooo-aw!"

Joel's father was singing at the top of his voice:

The farmer comes to town
With his wagon broken down
The farmer is the man who
feeds them all!

The pigs looked at Joel through the bars of the fence, their tiny eyes bright. "Oh-eee-eee!" They shook the snow from them and scampered into their house.

The dog barked, "Rarf!"

Joel's father waved at Joel and laughed. "The black cow had a calf."

Joel shouted, but he didn't laugh back, "Who always goes to bed with his shoes on!"

"I don't know," his father called, turning away, "but it's a spotted calf."

Joel told himself the answer, "A horse."

Joel plodded in the drifts on the road, going to the woods. "The tracks I am making are the first on this snow," he thought. A bird was telling about the storm, "Ah! Bob-white, ah!"

The white covered Joel's shoulders and the new cap. He went past the shed where his brother's goats and ducks lived. The goats put their front feet up on the gate. "Eh-eh-eh-eh-eh!" they said to Joel.

The ducks waddled about. They talked to themselves, "Quah-quah-quah."

Joel didn't even look at them. They were his brother's. Joel had nothing of his own. He scooped up snow and pressed it into a ball in his mittens. He was going to throw it at something!

Then Joel looked up in the sky. The snowflakes fell on his face. He heard a faraway goose gabble, high and shrill. Right after came a popping noise that meant hunters were shooting at the geese.

Joel knew that his father in the barnyard heard the hunters. His father would shake his fist in their direction.

"No hunters can shoot on our farm," Joel whispered, as the big birds came on, the long-necked wild geese from the northern nest grounds, going south to the feeding fields. In front was the leader. The others followed in two lines making a *V*.

"Honk! Onk, honk!" cried the leader.

"Kwonk," said those in the rear.

They flew low because of the snow-filled sky, looking for a place to land. Joel could hear the swishing of their wings. He stood not moving, not throwing his snowball, while the bobwhite called. Joel was hoping the geese would land in his father's fields.

He said softly, "No hunters allowed on our farm."

Then he saw the wounded one, staggering alone across the stormy sky. It was far behind the others. It flapped on one wing, down and then up, making no sound. The *V* of the flock came together in one line. Like a snake it went winding away in the snowy sky, the birds still gabbling.

Joel's eyes were on the one left behind. "It is coming down into my father's woods!"

When the trees hid it from him, Joel dropped his snowball and hurried. He walked through the trees. He walked all around the paths for a long time. He could not find the wild goose. The blue jays followed and screamed with a noise like two plates being hit

together. A crow shouted, "Baw! Baw!"

But where was the wild goose?

Then Joel saw the big bird, stone-still beside a bush, one button eye fixed on Joel. Its head and long thick neck were black, except for a white chin band that came up to each ear. Its body was gray-brown, its breast gray-white. Its eye glared at Joel.

He went toward it slowly. Just as he reached the bush, it cried "Kwonk," and spread its wings.

It ran, the broken wing dragging. Its long legs were strong.

Joel followed, panting, "Stop, Wild Goose!"

The goose went winding among the trees, skidding and sliding in the snow. It flapped and yelled, "Honk!"

The trees were close together. When the goose slipped, Joel hurled himself upon it.

The great wings beat and scratched his face. Joel wondered if he were strong enough to

hold the bird. It was a yard long and half as big as Joel. The broad beak closed upon his hand and only his wool mittens kept him from being hurt. Joel pushed the wings together against the goose's side. His arms closed about the warm wild bird.

It gave up. Joel lifted it. The goose stopped crying, and hissed, and then sighed. The long black neck hung down over Joel's arm.

Joel carried it out of the woods. His old foot tracks on the road were covered up by the white flakes.

Joel said, "Wild Goose, let me take care of you."

Joel took it to the shed where Jim's two goats and four ducks lived. He opened a gate and went into a corner pen. He closed the gate and put the goose down.

It flapped away from Joel, as far as the wall, and stood facing it. The broken wing touched the ground.

Joel brought a bucket of water and shelled grains of corn in the straw. The goose would not look or eat. Joel went outdoors where the goats and ducks were.

"Maaa, eh-eh-eh!" they said. "Quah, Quah."

"Hush," Joel told them and peeked inside. His goose had turned around. It was nibbling the corn and drinking the water. The empty feeling in Joel was filled and he stopped being lonely.

He grabbed for snow and packed

it into balls. He hit every tree he aimed for all the way home! He shouted:

I wished a wish, a great big wish
And the wish I wished came true!

His mother was putting dinner on the table. His father was washing his hands. Joel hung his coat and cap and kicked off his galoshes. He went to the sink. He rubbed soap on his hands.

His father said, "Did you see the geese flying, Joel?"

"Yes."

"Are you still feeling sad, Joel?" said his mother.

Father said, "The hunters were shooting at the geese."

"Hunters are bad," said Mother softly to her cat.

Father said, "Goose feathers are thick and strong. It is hard to hurt a flying goose."

Mother said, "Did the wild geese get away?"

"Yes," said Father.

"All but one," said Joel. His eyes were bright as stars.

They looked at him. "What did you say?"

"One came down in our woods," said Joel.

"That's too bad," said Father. "We'll never find it. But I'll go and look for it."

"When I was a little girl," Mother said, "a wild goose was shot down on my father's farm. We took care of it. In spring it was well. It flew off with a band when they came over."

Joel looked at her. "No!"

Mother put her cat down. She began to dish out the soup. "Every spring the goose came back to visit us."

"How did you know it was the same goose?" Father asked.

"It had a scar on its neck," Mother said.

Joel said, "My goose will not fly away. I'll lock it up!"

They turned to him. Mother said, "Did you catch the goose?"

"He isn't strong enough," Father said. "Joel couldn't."

"And I put it in Jim's shed."

"Well, what do you know!" Father said.

Joel ate his dinner. He went back outside. The snow had stopped falling. All the world was white.

The barns and sheds wore coats and tall hats of snow. In the pen the wild goose was cleaning its hurt wing. It plucked the feathers with its beak. It hissed at Joel and turned its back on him.

"Here, Wild Goose." Joel threw it a cookie he had brought along in his pocket. The bird jumped, as if frightened.

Joel went away. My wild goose is lonely. It is empty inside. Its wing hurts, too.

The next day Joel's father came to look at the bird. "The broken wing will be all right. It will heal."

By the end of the week the goose ate a cookie Joel threw in the straw. After another week the goose let Joel come into the pen. It took corn grains out of Joel's hand with its big beak.

The bird and the boy liked each other. One day Joel opened the pen door. "Come and take a walk, Wild Goose."

The sun shone golden as the goose walked past the goats and the ducks. The goose followed Joel up the road. It went in the tracks of Joel's galoshes.

They went past the barnyard. Joel's brother Jim and Father shouted and waved. The cows and the spotted calf and the pigs and the dog stared. The chickens came out of their coop to look.

Joel and the wild goose walked into the kitchen. Mother's cats ran under the table and chairs.

The bird stayed close to Joel. Mother gave each of them a cookie, and they went outside again.

After that day the two were always together. Joel talked to the goose, and it answered him in goose gabble, "Wa-wa-wa-wa-wa!"

The days and the weeks and the months went by. Spring came. Tiny green leaves unfolded. Thick-stemmed wood flowers woke and bloomed. The wind blew warm and smelled sweet.

Joel ran barefoot. Father began

to plow the fields. One of Jim's goats had a brown baby kid. Joel had a birthday.

His brother Jim said, "I will give you my baby kid."

Joel said, "No, thank you, Jim. I have Wild Goose."

Then Joel asked a riddle. "Why does a goat walk over a hill?"

Jim said, "Everyone knows. Because it can't walk under it!"

One day Joel was watching his father plowing. His goose was beside him in the field. He heard the

faraway wild geese gabbling in the sky. The wild birds were coming back!

Joel watched his goose. It lifted its head and looked up. It walked forward, its eyes on the sky. It opened its big wings and flapped them.

Joel was afraid. His arms went about his bird. "Don't go," he cried. "No!"

He held the goose tightly. The band of birds went over. They were gone. Joel took his arms away from his goose. It stood with head down. Joel knew it was feeling sad again.

The next day at breakfast, Mother left the door open so the spring could come into the room. There was no wind. All the birds in the land were singing.

"Today the wild geese will be flying," Mother said.

Father said, "They fly a thousand miles a day when it's like this!"

Joel couldn't talk. He walked out of the house and past the barns. He was in a hurry.

All the animals called to Joel. He wouldn't look at them. He ran and ran. He came to the shed where his goose lived with the goats and the brown baby kid and the ducks.

Joel got an ear of corn and fed his goose from his hand. Then he opened the gate. The two went down the road. The goose followed Joel's bare feet.

In a big open field Joel sat down. The bird was by his side. His arm was around it.

"I love you, Wild Goose," Joel said.

And the goose loved him. "Wa-wa-wa-wa-wa," it said.

They sat there for a long time, waiting. Late in the morning the

wild geese began to come over. Sometimes there were many flocks in the sky at a time. Their gabbling came soft and loud and then soft, as they neared and passed over and then were gone.

The goose beside Joel cried, "Kwonk, honk."

Joel took his arm away from it and stood up. The goose ran forward, looking into the sky.

The wild goose turned around. It looked at Joel. Its button eyes were bright.

Joel said, "Fly, Wild Goose! Don't be afraid."

The bird ran on its strong legs and flapped its wings. With a great rushing noise it went up into the air toward the band of geese.

The leader called to it, "Honk!"

And the wild goose cried back, "Kwonk!"

Joel shouted, "Come back next spring, Wild Goose!" It didn't have a scar on its neck, but Joel would know it!

And it answered Joel, "Kwonk."

The band flew away under the sun to the north. Joel watched. They grew smaller and smaller. They were gone. Joel was alone.

He heard a redbird singing about speckled eggs. Goldfinches went past, whistling about green leaves and brown nests.

Joel was walking down the road toward the shed. His brother Jim's goats and ducks were in the yard. The brown baby kid was running around. "Beh-eh-eh," it said.

Joel went in and picked up the brown baby kid. It was soft and warm. It was almost as big as a wild goose. He asked the mother goat, "What's more comical than a baby kid?"

Joel didn't feel empty inside. He wasn't lonely or sad. Part of the great wild bird would always be with Joel. And part of Joel was flying up north, high above the earth, on strong healed wings.

He told the mother goat the answer, "Two baby kids!"